THE BARKING BALLAD

A BARK-ALONG
MEOW-ALONG
BOOK

JULIE PASCHKIS

Atheneum Books for Young Readers
NEW YORK LONDON TORONTO SYDNEY NEW DELHI

A
atheneum

ATHENEUM BOOKS FOR YOUNG READERS
An imprint of Simon & Schuster Children's Publishing Division
1230 Avenue of the Americas, New York, New York 10020
© 2021 by Julie Paschkis
Text on pages 16–19 based on "An Elegy on the Death of a Mad Dog" by Oliver Goldsmith
Book design © 2021 by Simon & Schuster, Inc.

For information about special discounts for bulk purchases, please contact Simon & Schuster
Special Sales at 1-866-506-1949 or business@simonandschuster.com.
The Simon & Schuster Speakers Bureau can bring authors to your live event. For more
information or to book an event, contact the Simon & Schuster Speakers Bureau at
1-866-248-3049 or visit our website at www.simonspeakers.com.
The text for this book was set in Golden Cockerel ITC.
The illustrations for this book were rendered in watercolors.
Manufactured in China
0621 SCP
First Edition
2 4 6 8 10 9 7 5 3 1
Library of Congress Cataloging-in-Publication Data
Names: Paschkis, Julie, 1957– author, illustrator.
Title: The barking ballad : a bark-along, meow-along book / Julie Paschkis.
Description: First edition. | New York : Atheneum Books for Young Readers, [2021] | Audience:
Ages 4–8. | Summary: "A rhyming 'bark-along' and 'meow-along' picture book about dogs, cats,
and the sounds they make, following a cat and dog who become fast friends in a town of many
dogs—both mongrel, puppy, whelp, and hound, and curs of low degree!"—Provided by publisher.
Identifiers: LCCN 2020033621 | ISBN 9781534492608 (hardcover) | ISBN 9781534492615 (eBook)
Subjects: CYAC: Stories in rhyme. | Dogs—Fiction. | Cats—Fiction. | Friendship—Fiction. |
Animal sounds—Fiction.
Classification: LCC PZ8.3.P2716 Bar 2021 | DDC [E]—dc23
LC record available at https://lccn.loc.gov/2020033621

This is a bark-along, meow-along book.

Here's how you do it:

Whenever you see a red circle ●, *bark!*
You can yip, arrf, grrr, bow-wow,
or make any sound that a dog makes.

Whenever you see a yellow diamond ◆, *meow!*
You can mew, mrraww, yowl, purr,
or make any sound that a cat makes.

In memory of
Hazel Koenig

Good people here of every sort,
come listen to my song—

for like a corgi it is short,

and like a dachshund, long.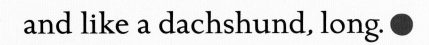

In our small town a cat was left
when someone moved away.
She wandered hungry and bereft

without a place to stay. ◆

She hid amidst the bushes low

and in the grasses tall.

No one watched her come or go—
the cat so swift and small.

And in that town

a dog was found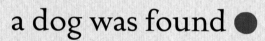

as many dogs there be

both mongrel ●

puppy ●

whelp ● and hound ●

and curs of low degree.

This dog explored the grasses green
with both his snout and eye.

The cat could sense that she was seen
as days and weeks went by.

One day a rock fell from above
and knocked the dog near dead. ●

With tender tongue and gentle love
the cat repaired his head.

The dog lay still with mournful sighs
while kitty worked her ways.

At last he opened up his eyes
and she returned his gaze.

The dog and cat became fast friends.
They traveled paw by paw.

If you looked out for one of them,

the pair was what you saw.

Soon the spaniel, sheepdog, poodle, ●
beagle, bulldog, collie, ●
borzoi, pug, and labradoodle ●
learned the cat was jolly. ◇

And in that town the dogs do bark
as dogs will do—and how!

A hundred barks ring through the park

Oliver Goldsmith was an Irish novelist, playwright,
and poet. He lived from 1728 to 1774. He wrote
the poem "An Elegy on the Death of a Mad Dog."
Like a dog stealing a bone, I took the fourth stanza
of his poem, which I loved as a child:

And in that town a dog was found,
As many dogs there be,
Both mongrel, puppy, whelp, and hound,
And curs of low degree.

Then I built my own poem around it,
using the rhythms of the original poem.
Many thanks to Oliver Goldsmith!

and one small stray meow. ◆